Bumblebees on water skis

Russell Punter

Illustrated by David Semple

Miss Honey's class of bumblebees
has come to Seaweed Bay.

They've got to study lots of rocks.

"This is SO dull," they say.

It's time to eat.

Miss Honey sounds quite stern.

Lee sees a sign along the beach.
"Free ski rides here today!"

Beetle's Skis

Free ski rides
here today!

3 minute trips
around the bay.

The bees have never skied before.

At first they shake and sway.

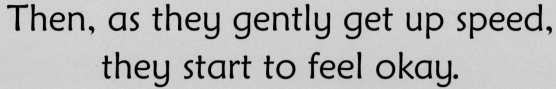

Then, as they gently get up speed,
they start to feel okay.

But when the driver makes a turn,
the sun shines in his eyes.

He steers the speedboat way off course.

"I can't see straight!" he cries.

They zoom across a sandy bank.

The bumblebees hold tight.

Soon sand is shooting through the air.
It's quite a crazy sight.

The speedboat bounces off the hull.

"What's that?" the captain shouts.

The boat lands, splash, back in the sea.

Uh oh! The bees let go!

But now they're heading for the shore.

The water skis stick in the sand.

The bees fly through the air.

They land up where they started from,
all dizzy from their scare.

Just then, Miss Honey reappears.
She's looking really pleased.

Starting to read

Even before children start to recognize words, they can learn about the pleasures of reading. Encouraging a love of stories and a joy in language is the best place to start.

About phonics

When children learn to read in school, they are often taught to recognize words through phonics. This teaches them to identify the sounds of letters that are then put together to make words. An important first step is for children to hear rhymes, which help them to listen out for the sounds in words.

You can find out more about phonics on the Usborne website at **usborne.com/Phonics**

Phonics Readers

These rhyming books provide the perfect combination of fun and phonics. They are lively and entertaining with great story lines and quirky illustrations. They have the added bonus of focusing on certain sounds so in this story your child will soon identify the long *e* sound, as in **bee** and **ski.** Look out, too, for rhymes such as **bay** – **say** and **air** – **scare.**

Reading with your child

If your child is reading a story to you, don't rush to correct mistakes, but be ready to prompt or guide if needed. Above all, give plenty of praise and encouragement.

Edited by Lesley Sims
Designed by Hope Reynolds

Reading consultants: Alison Kelly and Anne Washtell

First published in 2022 by Usborne Publishing Ltd., Usborne House, 83-85 Saffron Hill,
London EC1N 8RT, England. usborne.com Copyright © 2022 Usborne Publishing Ltd. The name
Usborne and the Balloon logo are Trade Marks of Usborne Publishing Ltd. All rights reserved.
No part of this publication may be reproduced, stored in a retrieval system or transmitted
in any form or by any means without the prior permission of the publisher. UE.